Zuzu's Petals

ISBN Black and White Edition: 978-1-943170-14-2

ISBN Color Edition: 978-1-943170-15-9

All Images: Mallory Jarot © 2016

Cover and Interior Design: Jane L Carman

Typefaces: Garamond, Courier, Arial, and Scribblings

Scribblings font courtsey of Michael Johnsen

Published by: Lit Fest Press, Carman, 688 Knox Road 900 North, Gilson, Illinois 61436

There are no rules.

festivalwriter.org

Zuzu's Petals

Jeff Jarct

for my family

Zuzu's Petals

I pull up and exit my vehicle.

In order to reach the building from the parking lot, which is an obscene distance from the school, I cross a bridge that suspends a small body of water that is barely frozen.

A transparent wafer of ice covers the surface of the water.

Only in the movies would someone be able to safely hop across its surface, Gene Kelly-like, without breaking through to experience hypothermia's bitter embrace.

Without realizing it, I have stopped in the middle of the bridge, head down, hands clasped.

When I finally look up, my watering eyes decipher a man and a woman holding hands.

They offer me a sidelong glance. Their crystal orbs scream, "What is *that* guy's problem?"

I follow their silhouettes like a humiliated shadow towards the welcoming light of the school.

Even though my mind has already jumped from the side of the bridge to its early death, my feet follow the receding figures in their shared wake towards the building in which Zuzu's holiday program awaits.

I'm not ashamed to say that I, Jules, prefer Fiction to Reality.

Fiction will become the Official Reality of record.

Julie and I are still together.

Zuzu will always be my little girl.

We are a happy family and always will be.

Something's wrong with mommy and daddy.

They won't tell me what.

Butterflies in my stomach are making babies.

Butterflies being born every second.

Wait a minute.

Butterflies are worms before they're even butterflies.

Maybe I have worms in my stomach.

Maybe I have worms *and* butterflies.

There's lots of people out there.

There's mommy.

I want to go on.

Where's daddy?

I'm here.

I enter the building. To my right is a chiffarobe-sized glass display case. Back in the day it housed two plaques that meant something to me. Amidst the militarily-precise rows and columns of dusty rectangles of gold, my own name was etched for pseudo-eternity, quasi-memorialized in half-inch capital block letters. These plaques and others like them were long ago removed from the case to make room for future elementary school alumni, my scholarly descendants, and the old, irrelevant plaques no doubt were burned in a bonfire or sent to decompose in a landfill or a graveyard especially designed for the purpose. Who knows?

The gymnasium in which the holiday program will be performed hasn't changed much. You don't relocate a huge, cavernous indoor expanse like that if you can help it. Why would you want to? It hasn't been refurbished, which adds to my feeling of having been transported through time, if not for the ubiquitous presence of camcorders, smart phones, digital cameras, and all manner of electronic device.

My mind courses back to 1981. The school administration has decided to shut off the heat to the gym in an attempt to prevent random upchucks and faintings. This executive decision results in a Celsius reading inside the gym that is consistent with the interior of a walk-in freezer on the ice-planet Hoth. I feel the tingle of goose pimples metastasize on my forearms like pinhead tumors with arm hairs standing erect at attention when I enter the maw of the gym's gaping wooden double-doors.

But it is the present, and the temperature, like everything else in my life, is luke-warm.

Julie, sometimes you have to call a spade a spade, and sometimes you have to call bullshit bullshit. Sometimes you have to leave your husband out of self-respect. Truth be told, your life with him has consisted of entirely too much bullshit. You've been forced for all practical purposes to *inhale* it for the past decade. Stop doing that. Hold my hand and breathe out.

I am, David. I'm trying to exhale...

The man's vocabulary is fucking pompous, pretentious, and arrogant. Nobody knows what he's saying. Nobody uses the words that he does. The shit he says only appears in old, dusty books that no one reads anymore.

David, please. I'm going to miss Zuzu's number...

Your soon-to-be ex-husband is a fucking fossil. His mind is fossilized.
I wish we could be alone...
right now...

Zuzu is my daughter. I need to be here. I shouldn't be texting during the program. And, truth be told, Jules isn't all bad. Otherwise I wouldn't have fallen in love with him...

Look, I'm erudite and educated and all that stuff. But at least I know how to talk to people. And I know how to treat *you*...

Yes, you're right...

I want you. You're so heavy. It's going to be the way things used to be. We can press the reset button on our lives and start over from where we left off when we were younger...

The past isn't dead. It isn't even past...

Quoting the Beatles and Faulkner in a single text? Now you're sounding just like Jules...

Jesus, don't say that...

Jesus, what I would do to be a kid again. These kids don't know how easy they have it.

The annual elementary school dramatic-musical extravaganza usually consists of both select instrumental and choral performances. A cranberry-colored partition that separates the music room from the gym is cracked open and retracted to accommodate all the performers. The band students and those, like my Zuzu, who are performing piano selections, are housed in the music room. There is a set of risers in the shape of a crescent moon knocked on its side near the front of the makeshift stage. Here the students who are singing can belt out carols in cacophonous unison.

When I was a student here, the overcast-sky floor tiles and bright yellow lines demarcating the basketball court dimensions always reminded me of elongated and curving blocks of lemon-meringue filling floating on top of speckled, dirty dishwater. The canary-colored rectangles didn't undulate but rather were motionless, as if the grey liquid was in a calm pool undisturbed by wind. I recall pretending that these lines and dashes were haven-like, foot-sized islands and tightropes of safety strung across the stormcloud-colored boiling waters that seethed just below. Black streaks courtesy of various student gym footwear stops and starts and scuffs and slides floated on the surface. They are still floating there, but my mind tells my body that it is too old to spring out of its seat to see if its skills at hopping across the tiled maelstrom have suffered across the chasm of the intervening decades.

The squiggly nature of the design of the room's ceiling tiles always reminded me of unwieldy piles of spaghetti on a tuxedo-black background, as if gravity had been reversed and, were it to be restored, I would tumble headlong into piles of pasta that would cushion the fall. The ceiling is held up by bone-white girders.

This forces me to contemplate the invisible girders that hold up life.

They can crumble at any moment, like they are memories made of mist, misremembered.

In my long-deceased elementary school day, in this very building, during this particular breed of holiday program that I am about to witness as a member of the audience, the heater would be running full blast to counter the early-December outside elements. Combined with the formidable number of teachers, students, and proud parents packed into the enclosed space like superheated sardines boiling in their own juices, this made for extremely sweltering conditions. Not a holiday season would go by without a handful of spotlit students succumbing to the intense heat, fainting and tumbling off the risers or, worse, becoming physically ill and losing their noon repast the hard way.

The lights dim and the program starts. In the gloaming I can make out the empty rack where battleship-grey folding chairs will need to be racked upside-down one after the other post-program. I am already anticipating the end.

Zuzu is the very first student to perform. She plays a simple rendition of "O Christmas Tree" that is free of complicated chord structures. I've heard variations of the piece off and on for the last couple months, smooth patches interrupted by avant-gardish interludes of sudden discordant musical constructs produced by Zuzu's frustration.

Back in our homestead, hearing her work her way through these microcosmic struggles, I felt the water wells of my eyes fill up, and I'm afraid that presently they are on the verge of overflowing their teary juices like aggressively-squeezed orbs of fruit. These homegrown rivulets will be recognized immediately by the strangers surrounding me. Forthwith when they recall this event I'll be remembered as "that strange stranger with the tear-stained face. Remember that poor, sorry bastard? What was his problem?"

I notice a smattering of fallen, shriveling, probably dying crimson-with-a-blight-of-brown poinsettia leaves garnishing the polished ebony top of the piano on which Zuzu is playing. Her performance is followed by that of an olive-skinned student with a bowl haircut clad in a black T-shirt emblazoned with the large, ivory, block letters "FBI" (I discover upon closer examination after the recital they stand for "Female Body Inspector"). He clutches a French horn to his belly and farts and splurts his way through what I think is Alan Silvestri's theme from *The Polar Express*. The lad sounds like an out-board boat motor that is running out of gas. Performing next is a scrum of chittering first graders who, after stomping up and across the risers, belt out a wildly-out-of-tune rendition of "Silent Night." The young ones commence the second chorus, murmuring with not nearly the confidence the first verse exuded.

Midway through the next selection, I hear liquid splatting onto tile, followed by EEEEEEEWWWWWWWWWWWWWWWWW!!!!!

It is just enough to cause my lips to curve up at the edges. Tears pause at the preci-pice of my lower eyelids, and they decide to not jump off the cliff.

God, oh God, it's starting.

In my lap, a bouquet of flowers for Zuzu lies wilting. It is an assortment of white, pink, and red roses.

My and Julie's given names have always served as a trigger for much mirth and comment between friends and new acquaintances alike. The similarity of the monikers our respective parents gave us has caused many a colleague to comment that Julie's and my high-school romance, college courtship, and subsequent marriage was pre-ordained, inscribed in the stars and planets whirling above.

Star-cross'd lovers, indeed.

Utter garbage, when all was said and done.

Well, it would be more accurate to say that it's in the process of being done.

The man's fucking addicted to movies, *that* movie in particular..

You seem to be hell-bent on placing the word 'fuck' in any conversation that we have...

Hey, I can't help it. I'm a schoolteacher. The word 'fuck' permeates the air of every public institution of learning in America. It's in movies, it's bleeped out on reality TV, it's in everyday chats, forums. It's in the very oxygen we breathe.

So long as you don't use that word in front of Zuzu...

I'll fucking try.

That's not remotely funny, David.

I'm sorry, honey. Seriously, though. There is nothing worse than somebody who refuses to move forward in their life, like their feet are stuck in a puddle of Super Glue...

Don't I know it...

I'm perched on a weatherworn picnic table, a collection of splinters dappled with rust-colored paint, held together by the inertia of time. It's unreasonably warm for December 10th, and Zuzu is sprinting from the table to a beanbag-chair-sized mound of damp leaves the color of cranberries and black-bean soup.

The innocence of youth. How to get back to it?

Yet the doomsday clock on her innocence is speedily, inexorably winding down to zero. I'll have to break the news to her very soon. But I don't want to do it alone.

December 8ᵗʰ now will be a day that will live in personal infamy for me for two distinct reasons. Not only is it the day that John Lennon was assassinated, but I'll now also recall it for much more crushing, personal reasons.

The events of a couple days ago run like one of those John Hughes-ish '80s movie montages sans a Simple Minds or Harold Faltermeyer soundtrack. I see a series of innocuous images from that day—Zuzu's youth indoor soccer league, fast-food repast at McDonalds, erecting and trimming the artificial Christmas tree at home. This pastiche bleeds to Julie dropping the bombshell that for weeks had no doubt been festering in her.

The memories and emotions and impulses from that day are still fresh. I'm folding bathroom towels in the master bedroom, I-pod buds in my ears, listening to the strains of Joe Walsh's "Life's Been Good" to alleviate my mundane chore when Julie strides into the room. I can still see her motion to me to turn off my music as she settles in the chair in the corner of the bedroom as if she is an empress on the verge of pronouncing a royal edict.

I love you, but I don't love you quite enough to stay married to you.

I have Zuzu sequestered downstairs watching a *Spongebob Squarepants* holiday episode.

We've been having problems for a long time...This has never been a partnership...We've slowly been drifting apart...You need to grow up and be more responsible and practical about real things in the real world that really matter.

Shocked but not rendered speechless, I immediately suggest the usual banal remedies—moving to a different house, taking a vacation, attending church more regularly, renewed marriage vows, couple's counseling.

I've met someone else. Actually, I've reconnected with someone else.

Who?

It doesn't matter.

Doesn't matter? Seriously? Who is it? It's not David, is it?

Yes. It's David.

David. Dammit. Why?

I just told you.

What about Zuzu? How will she be able to understand? She's only a first grader. I can't believe this is happening.

She'll understand. I was in first grade when my parents divorced, and I turned out to be normal.

Well, that's certainly debatable, isn't it? How long have you been messing up our lives with this virtual fantasy of yours?

My fantasy? You have the gall to accuse me of messing up our lives with my fantasy? What about your fantasies, plural?

Dammit, I asked you how long has this been going on?

Deflecting my questions and ignoring your role in this, huh? Whatever. Two or three months. We found each other on Facebook. Re-discovered each other, actually.

You found him or he found you?

I found him.

I don't believe this. This is uncanny.

I hate it when you use big words like "uncanny."

How about we separate for a spell and take things from there?

No.

You're sure?

Yes.

What do we say to Zuzu?

We just tell her that we don't feel the same way about each other anymore. But we still love her and always will.

But *I* still love *you*. I'm mad as hell at you right now, but I still love you. And you just told me that you still loved me. I know we've had our problems. But I still want this to work. I love you.

If I said the same back to you, I'd be lying.

So you're saying that you just lied to me a moment ago?

Jules. Please.

I hope that you're not looking for perfection with him because you won't find it.

I'm not looking for perfection. I know that life isn't perfect. I'm just looking for something different.

Oh, it'll be different, all right. But what will we tell Zuzu?

I already told you what we tell her.

I can't do that. It'll crush her.

You never have *been good at dealing with things in the real world that need to be dealt with. You're always reading too many books and watching too many movies and spacing out. That's all you do when you sit in that favorite chair of yours. You avoid reality and responsibility in your little closed-off world.*

But I *need* the escape. Everyone needs their own personalized brand of respite to get away from the things they don't want to think about or deal with.

"Respite?" Who the hell uses *words like that when they're arguing with someone?*

This is hardly a regular conversation.

Just you, Jules. You're a total egghead. Which has always been part of the problem. You can't communicate, and you still just spend too much time outside the real world. It's really gotten to be too much for me. Too much.

I know, Julie. I know. I'll try to be better.

It's too late for that, Jules.

It's not fair to Zuzu. Little kids deserve the largest bubble of innocence at the start of their lives that they can possibly get. Your stubbornness, your refusal to fix this, is totally going to break that bubble.

It's you *who needs his bubble of innocence broken. We have to tell her sometime, and the sooner the better.*

I refuse to do that. I'm not ready to tell her. I'm certain we can work all this out.

Jules, I'm getting the hell off the Titanic while there's still room in a lifeboat. You worship the damn past too much. The world has moved on. There are easier ways to do things. And I firmly believe that I love actual life more than you do.

The days of my life churn in my mind like grains of sand beneath rolling, incessant waves. I want Zuzu's tinier footprints to be right there in the fresh unmarked sand next to mine as we stride forward.

I drop the needle on a copy of the Beach Boys' *Pet Sounds* I just acquired from Waiting Room Records. The Brian Wilson-penned harmonies tease and taunt me.

I keep looking for a place to fit

Where I can speak my mind

I've been trying hard to find the people

That I won't leave behind

I am resigned to the fact that I'm nothing if not a lost cause. The fact that I'm listening to said song on a turntable highlights my plight, my inability to swim out of the old-school current in which I'm trapped. Yet vinyl *has* made comeback of sorts for audiophiles, they say. And dammit, given that, why should I feel strange if I still prefer to read physical books as well? Why the devil do I have to perform some kind of army crawl past the employees at a bookstore who are hawking the latest version of some electronic reading device and causing their jobs to make that slow swirl down the toilet of oblivion in the process? Isn't it the content that matters anyways? Whether I listen to *Rubber Soul* on vinyl or CD or 8-track or a download, what does it matter? The greatness of the album will never change.

I cannot help myself. Like Brian Wilson, I feel as if I was born in the wrong era. And I hate a good portion of myself for it. I don't understand why I was conceived and birthed and raised in the very same decade that spawned Watergate and Jimmy Carter and disco and 8-tracks and…well…*Star Wars*.

Yet why do people nowadays feel compelled to take pictures of food they've either prepared or consumed? Why do they post innermost feelings that should be reserved for *real-life* moments of intimacy with another living, *present* human being? Because now they can ponder what to say and type it without uncomfortable, pregnant patches of silence and interminable stretches of waiting for a response and the glassy stares of the other person in a conversation in the *Now*, boring their own crystal orbs deep into the soul of another.

Simply stated, if you don't post it on Facebook or tweet about it nowadays, the event or thought doesn't and didn't happen because no one has read about it and seen the carefully-composed pictures and commented on them or otherwise enjoyed them. Hence, those events and thoughts that represent a life never occurred.

None of this is nourishing in any way for anyone. It's like eating candy corn for breakfast, lunch, and dinner day after day after day.

Was the secret to marry someone who had the very same obsessions that I have? How possible is that? Or maybe someone who obsesses on completely different things but at the same levels of intensity that I do? Did I fail to follow the dictum that opposites attract? Do opposites even attract? I think maybe all they end up doing is pissing each other off. Or one person becomes colossally pissed while the other glides along.

Like me.

I look around the darkened gymnasium, and I see all manner of Smartphone and camcorder, some of which I recognize from Best Buy ads over the years, LED displays reflected in eyeglasses, the technological equivalent of lighters at a rock concert, digital lightning bugs with occasional stage whispers bubbling to the surface…

Sony Handycam HDR-CX260V 16GB HD Flash Memory Camcorder Model # HDR-CX260/LI 30x optical / 350x digital zoom; up to 8.9 MP still image mode; 3" Xtra Fine LCD touch-screen display; low-light recording; optical SteadyShot image stabilization press 'Record' now honey I'm recording Sony Bloggie Live 8GB Flash Memory Camcorder Model # MHSTS55/S Video streaming via Wi-Fi; compact design; 12.8 MP digital still images; 3" touch-screen LCD; low-light recording; SteadyShot image stabilization; 4x digital zoom I wish those bastards in front of us would cut out the fucking talking JVC Wi-Fi HD Flash Memory Camcorder Model # GZEX210BUS 40x optical/200x digital zoom don't say fuck or bastard out loud honey we're at a grade school holiday concert 1920 x 1080 digital still mode; 3" touch screen; night recording; image stabilization; Wi-Fi I want to post this as soon as we get home honey Samsung Flash Memory Camcorder Model # H300 HD 30x optical/300x digital zoom; 4.9MP still image capture; 3" touch screen LCD; optical image stabilization don't talk while I'm filming You're ruining it honey Samsung HD Flash memory Camcorder Model # QF20 Wi-Fi 20x optical/30x digital zoom; 1.75MP digital still mode; low-light recording; OIS Duo plus image stabilization; built-in Wi-Fi Godbles-sit you just ruined it Fuck it now we'll just have to delete the whole goddamned recording

...Technology, I think to myself, is like running to board a bus that you will never be able to catch.

The nooks and crannies in my finished basement are crammed with old-school newsprint that day by day, week by week, month by month, becomes obsolete, the paper itself as a result of the damp cool pruning like the fingers of a child who's just exited a swimming pool. I read the successive editions of the newspaper as best I can, trying desperately to keep up with the deluge of news, trying to integrate perusing the stories into that day's schedule of chores and needs and leisure pursuits, only to cast all sections of the accumulating papers into a metastasizing pile of newsprint that before long comes up to Zuzu's forehead. It saddens me that I can never feel caught up with current events. As if that isn't bad enough, my DVR is nearly chock-full, I purchase DVDs that I never have the time to get around to watching for months and even years, remaining wrapped in cellophane and accumulating a thin sludge of dust, stored horizontally on a shelf next to the stacked pillar of papers that continue to breed and languish, the ends of the folded sections at the top curling and turning a grayish-yellow.

I want so desperately to be a sponge, but I'm afraid I'm a dried-up sponge, petrified, and lack the ability to soak up anything.

I lament the things in life that just seem to end without my being able to mentally prepare myself for them. This marriage would certainly qualify, but there are other things, truth be told, that have been more sacred to me in my life. One day you are watching a little one navigate the monkey bars at a playground, hand over hand, eyes with a laser-like focus ahead and above, anticipating that next grip of the bar, you the parent ensconced on a bench, nose epoxied to a newspaper or journal, trying off and on to focus yourself on the present in order to savor the moment that is already past. You then wake up one morning and you find yourself parked in a car across from that very same playground, and you realize that years, even decades have evaporated since you've had moments like that.

And the little ones have grown up. They are gone, and the moments too are gone, as these present moments during which I'm having these very thoughts are also already gone, barely visible in the rearview mirror.

Sometimes I feel that I'm the guy who's fucking everything up for everybody, including myself, but doesn't mean to.

It will forever bug me that magic the way I want it to be doesn't exist in the real world, at least the way that magic exists in the mind of a child. That's why I'm drawn to movies so much. Magic can happen there. And as pathetic as it may sound, I can forget for a time that I am witnessing an illusion. Even my adult self can pretend that it's real.

Jules, I don't think you have an adult self.

That's harsh, Julie.

Pretending is tricking yourself by another name.

I guess I'd rather trick myself than rub my face in negativity too much.

But then you're missing out on your own life. And it doesn't stop there. My life. Zuzu's life. Our shared life.

Life is what happens while you're busy making other plans.

What?

John Lennon wrote that. Actually he both wrote it and sang it.

I knew that already. And you're completely ignoring my point.

I feel sometimes like I'm married to Eeyore.

Okay, Christopher Robin.

Huh? Okay, okay. I know that at times you have to confront and accept what has happened to us, but it can be so damn hard.

Sometimes, Jules, you just have to confront and accept that we've grown up and we aren't the same people we used to be.

I'm having that goofy feeling again.

It's not that usual tingly there-are-butterflies-flapping-wildly-around-the-inside-of-my-stomach kind of feeling I usually have before I go out in front of people and perform.

I'm standing on the stage, well, actually at the side of the stage.

Am I real?

Maybe God or Jesus or somebody who isn't human is dreaming all of us.

Daddy once told me that he wished he dreamed in black and white.

I dream colors. I am in color.

I sometimes wake up at night and touch my chin and cheeks and nose and forehead.

I run my fingers down my own body, just to make sure that I'm here.

I also sometimes play this goofy game with myself.

I tell myself that I'm not really where I am, that I'm not really alive.

I just live in my imagination that isn't alive either.

And the car that I'm riding in on the road at night with mommy and daddy isn't here.

It's disappeared.

The light from the headlights goes out on the road, and I wonder.

I'm always wondering, wandering.

Zuzu and I are washing and drying dishes together. We are bumping our butts together in time to the music blasting from the stereo, some current hip-hop song that is mostly gobbledygook to my classic-rock ears. I faintly recognize it but can't identify it fully by correct artist and title. I am embarrassed to admit this to my daughter because I'm afraid that she will think I am even more of a hopeless old-school geek than she already does. This is silly. I should just cave in and ask her.

Julie and I used to do the dishes in this very fashion, mostly before we had Zuzu. On lucky nights our bumping and grinding butts would lead to the horizontal bumping and grinding that I now ache for. I would always go out of my way to put Billy Joel or James Taylor, two of Julie's favorite artists, on at a not-too-loud but discernible volume at the start of our clearing the table in desperate anticipation that this very thing would lead to inevitable hanky-panky. Sometimes it did, but never often enough.

I hold up the scrubbie I am using to wash with. It's encrusted with shit-brown dregs of Lord knows what, along with congealed globs of yellow cheese whitened by dishwater. Zuzu's nose wrinkles up as if I or the dog has just let loose some horrific flatus, and I mimic her expression, upping the exaggeration ante as much as I can. I sense an impromptu scrubbie funeral forthcoming.

You've been a good scrubbie, but you have to be retired, buried at landfill sea. Hasta la vista, baby…err, scrubbie.

You're silly, Daddy.

I look around as the program continues, employing the biological certainty of my own eyeballs. Most of the people surrounding me are viewing each moment through all manner of electronic viewfinder as I'm seeing and digesting visuals and aurals, and these other schmos are missing out on the actuality of everything as it happens.

How many digital copies of this single event shot from myriad angles do we need? Where are all these multiple copies of home movies going to go when we're all dead, buried, and gone? Certainly our distant future progeny isn't going to feel compelled to hold onto shelfloads of VHS tapes, DVDs, and hard drives filled to capacity with nondescript, relatively anonymous Christmas pageants, little league baseball games, junior high promotions, high school graduations, various school plays and musicals, and family vacation minutiae. Will even the museums of the future be interested in saving artifacts beyond count from an era so hyperconscious when it comes to preserving itself? It would be like going all-out, pulling out all the stops to preserve a single grain of sand that in 1985 had washed up on a random beach now lost to memory.

What are people going to think when *I* die? They'll be opening up all these Rubbermaid storage containers and shoeboxes of various sizes stuffed with trinkets and gewgaws and mementos that have enormous amounts of personal relevance for me and are impossible for me to discard, and people will take a long, puzzled look at the whole lot, and were I alive, and were I a resident of New York, I'd be signed, sealed, and delivered to Bellevue.

Zuzu is writing out her thank-you notes for her birthday gifts from myriad relatives. Her birthday occurs near the beginning of November. It is now the beginning of December. Once I get past my embarrassment at her procrastination (since it will suggest my own laziness as a parent, as it was my job as the dutiful paterfamilias to make sure she takes care of such responsibilities), I can't help but think of the proper protocol regarding them. When I was Zuzu's age, one of the reasons I loathed such formalities was that I thought that my initial, snail-mailed, handwritten, personalized thank-you card containing my scribbled gratitude on the envelope's Hallmark-brand innards would trigger a chain of correspondence that would fast career out of my control. Such a chain would stretch out into infinity, and I thought to myself, Will I receive a thank-you for the thank-you that I had originally generated, and will I then be forced by some quasi-ancient sense of decorum to then feel compelled to send yet another thank-you to the third power, so to speak, the process akin to looking into a mirror being echoed into a pool of infinite reflections, down to the end of time? Will I be sending out the latest in a string of thank-you's whose genesis stemmed from a small Bible I had received from an aunt for my First Communion? Would death, either hers or mine, sever the obligations of such a contract? This thought process naturally led to feelings of morbid remorse.

Nevertheless, I have used paternal force to suggest that Zuzu compose her thank-you cards the old-school way, which I'm pretty sure she resents with all her heart. She's told me multiple times that she can just send out a single e-card to everyone she needs to, which would be much, much easier and more colorful and would have all kinds of neat computer graphics and sound effects, but I still tell her no, that's not the proper way.

You're a fossil, Jules. You belong underground ossifying and sandwiched between two layers of rock. And you're a geek besides.

I will never be ashamed of being a geek. My definition of a geek is someone who likes or enjoys a certain thing way beyond the extent of a normal person.

Well, that definitely qualifies you as a geek then.

I know. I'm all sorts of different varieties of geek.

You were lucky. I put up with your geekiness for the longest time. I was the perfect spouse.

The perfect spouse. Yeah. The perfect spouse in hell. Lucifer's bride.

You have no idea, Jules.

my name is zuzu an im writing about a memrble expi-
rence for school an i lik 2 writ an daddys ben writin
2 an u r my favorit teacher so here goes

daddy use 2 giv mommy 3 difrent colur flowrs for the
day they met on feb 3 1 red 1 pink 1 whit i went
somtimes wit daddy to piggly wiggly an we stand for
minits lookin for flowrs that wernt 2 short or 2 long
or wrinkly or wit 2 many pedals fallin lik leavs fallin
off trees in fall but the leavs r brown an tan an
orang an yelow an red an some times still green not
whit or pink tho that wud b neat i like 2 jump in
them lik linus b4 he goes lookin 4 the great pumkin
but i dont jump in wit a suker lik he did an ther is
no pyano music

at piggly wiggly i wud pul them flowrs out the whit
plstik buckit wit a handl an filed wit watr dripin the
drops wet an i dont wan 2 stik miself wit no thrns

daddy an me tuk drivs in the stat park by r hous
wen mommy was workin on winde days wen brown an
tan an yelow leaves fall down from ceeder an pins
(daddy gav me thes tree names) in litl tornados he
stop the car leaves slid an flip down windoe we both
leav the car an walk th twistee turnee rode an my
hand is safe becuz of daddys big hand aroun mine
like a walnut shell aroun the stuf insid daddy lets
me pick my favorit yelow an red an brown an green
leave the pretiest 1 each

but in spring time when the flowrs on the trees fell down on r car an it was like confeti hitin the window lik whit rain daddy lets me turn on the wiprs like 2 robot arms daddy stops the car an we both got out an pikd up flowrs that stuk 2 the groun lik they wer glued ther i tell daddy i want red an pink 1s 2 go wit the whit 1s that they culd b lik mommys pedals he tels me that thes 1s wer speshal an that they r my pedals an i hol out my han that isnt ful o pedals an he taks 3 pedals 3 gud 1s an he tels me we can colur 1 red an 1 pink latr wen i tel him that my gud crayola markrs r in my desk at skool he says we hav 2 hav sum markrs an i says we only hav a hol bunch a 1s that r outve colurin juce all over the hous an daddy says dont wory that we can luk in the skool supply secshen in piggly wiggly on the way hom an I can hav a compleet set at r hous an at skool but that i hav 2 tak car of them anywho or I can git paynt

daddy stuk the 3 pedals in that smal pokit in his pants an askd me what movee is this from an i wantd to mak daddy hapy cuz that stuf maks daddy mak hapy smiles an so i say star wars daddy

an he say no it's a wonderful lif an I say yes daddy it can be an he says yes sometimz it is

Zuzu's Petals

I look out at Zuzu plunging into the leaves, and my eyes well up. I still feel traces of a throbbing ache that has metastasized in my gut since December 8th, the day of Julie's infamous pronouncement. Julie and I have been together for so long. Too much of my own past is intertwined with strands of hers, so much so that large portions of my individual-ized prior existence is tangled with hers and hence indistinguishable as just my own. I'm ashamed to say that I'm still feeding on the illusory hope that Julie and I'll be able to patch things up, so I've told Zuzu that Mommy's gone to visit Grandma and Grandpa because one of them is sick and that I don't quite know when she'll be back.

These lies I'm forcing myself to tell are killing me because I know they won't hold water for long. The cliché about kids seeing right through layers of adult bullshit is so true. Kids are too damn smart. They're certainly smarter than I am. It's only taken Zuzu a small handful of days to spark a skepticism mixed with concern that I fear will soon fan itself into an uncontrollable all-out dread, to be followed up by immediate anger and hurt at my deliberate fibbing.

The sky presently resembles dirty bathwater bleeding to gray. Yet I can distinguish occasional strobe-light flashes from within the bruised cloud formations that outline and highlight their shapes. An otherwise absent sun smears a dab of burnt orange above the horizon. December. Who on God's emerald earth ever heard of rain and thunder in the Midwest near the end of December? The globe *is* warming, life as we know it *is* ending…

I can make out the distant, faded disk of the moon, pockmarked with ashen con-tinents. God's flashlight. His porthole. At the moment I want nothing more than to be able to lasso it and pull it down for Zuzu. Time to go inside. Over Zuzu's grating protestations, I usher her indoors, the wooden screen door to the back porch slamming, the rusty latch secure.

Zuzu and I step across the threshold into the house. So much for a white Christ-mas. "It figures," I add aloud.

What, Daddy? Zuzu asks.

Nothing, pumpkin. Just talking to myself, that's all.

To our right is a stone fireplace that has always reminded me of an underground grotto. Inside burn the dregs of what a couple hours ago was a roaring conflagration. Dying embers still pulse in amber and russet tones. I know the fire doesn't jibe with the balmy tem-perature outside, yet it is but one sign of my stubbornness in relation to perceived adversity or the way I believe things should be.

In the opposite corner of the room, the TV shows *It's a Wonderful Life*. The film is an all-time favorite of mine, one of a few films that I can sit down and watch at any random point during its running time. Presently, I can tell at a glance that this particular broadcast has been running for roughly an hour. I'm such an aficionado of the film, in fact, that I cajoled Julie into naming our daughter Zuzu in honor of George Bailey's fictional progeny in the film. The confusion and disbelief that many people displayed when first learning our daughter's name never bothered me; I rather reveled in it. Some people immediately caught the reference; some didn't. The same could not be said for Julie at first. *It's like naming your kid Anakin or Obi-Wan or Jar-Jar*, she griped. I didn't tell her at the time that, being a *Star Wars* fan, I had considered Han and Luke and Ben for any forthcoming sons in the family. She gradually warmed to our daughter's quirky appellation.

I own several copies of *It's a Wonderful Life* in various formats, but there remains something special about catching one of the seasonal, biennial television broadcasts. When I was Zuzu's age, I loved catching similar showings of *The Wizard of Oz* and the Rankin-Bass version of *Rudolph the Red-Nosed Reindeer* on TV. Back then I remember sprinting to the kitchen for a hastily-assembled Louis Rich turkey, cheese, and Maytag bleu-cheese dressing sandwich and an orange. I would claw with impatience at the rind of the fruit during the lightning-quick commercial breaks so as not to miss a moment of the programs. Tonight I may have to settle for a DVD screening, but maybe, just maybe, I'll be able to catch the ending of the picture during its network broadcast. It's the best, most emotionally-gripping part of the movie anyway.

It's a Wonderful Life haunts my life. I have accumulated a plethora of gewgaws, knick-knacks, and other assorted memorabilia commemorating the film: coffee mugs, lobby cards, Hallmark Keepsake ornaments, a miniaturized ceramic recreation of the town of Bedford Falls that includes the Bailey Building and Loan, Mr. Gowers' Drug Store, the Bedford Falls public library, Martini's Bar, and, of course, George and Mary's residence at 320 Sycamore. I'm constantly prowling the Internet for enticing future purchases. Much of these items are proudly and prominently displayed in my first-floor study / office / computer room. Other items that I'm not able to display at Julie's insistence are housed in Rubbermaid containers piled one upon the other in the basement crawlspace.

I've learned the hard way that there are fine lines between obsession, eccentricity, and idiocy, and at this relatively late point in my dying marriage to Julie, I realize that I assumed incorrectly that she had accepted, however grudgingly, my many odd habits. It's now obvious that I've crossed one of these fine lines and that Julie is interested in seceding from our less-than-perfect union.

Perhaps I've crossed all of the fine lines at once.

It's now technically Zuzu's bedtime. As selfish as it sounds, watching *It's a Wonderful Life* would provide me with a much-desired escape from having to break the news of my and Julie's shipwrecked marriage to Zuzu. Yet I know that tonight I *have* to break the news to her. Over the course of the past couple of weeks, I've experienced the same regret one feels when holding on to some type of tragic news, whether it be that a loved one has a terminal illness or a friend has perished in a car accident, and the bearer of such tidings is forced to endure that time span during which the person who hasn't heard the news is full of bliss and unaware that he or she is on the cusp of life changing for the worse. My heart always breaks during such moments, moments similar to my present situation.

Upstairs, I settle in for Zuzu's ritual bedtime story. Leaning my head back to rest against the headboard of her bed, I have the familiar feeling that the back of my skull is flattening during our shared nightly reading exercise. I thumb open a picture book and begin reading aloud until Zuzu interrupts the flow of my narrative. While I relate to her a colorful two-page spread concerning various flying fauna, she begins.

Daddy, do birds hurt people?

Well, most people would say no, unless they're Alfred Hitchcock.

I gaze upwards through the slits in the Venetian blinds at the scattered lightning, bone-white cracklings from a heavenly campfire just outside the window. I also detect occasional red, blue, and orange aureoles from the walnut-sized Christmas bulbs that border the outside of Zuzu's bedroom window. The exterior lights, like the family Christmas tree in the living room downstairs, will come down after the holiday season has died and be stuffed away in the basement crawlspace until next year, hidden amidst my *It's a Wonderful Life* collectibles and other assorted paraphernalia. Julie, in a gently insulting way, characterized it as Jules' toys, quote-unquote. Yet in a backhanded way they hold untold meaning for me. If the preternaturally warm weather lasts, I'll have to take advantage of it to rip down the outside lights and decorations. Never quite as fun taking them down as putting them up. How especially true this year. I spy a clear glass of water residing on Zuzu's weathered, hand-me-down nightstand, along with a smattering of petals from a potpourri case she has recently raided.

Gliding her index finger across the page, Zuzu points out one bird in particular and looks up. *What about S-W-A-N?* She is proud of her automatic, vast knowledge of the alphabet. *Do they hurt people?*

No, they usually don't hurt anybody. Not in stories, anyways.

I didn't want to tell her about the swan's penchant for nipping at the fingers of little girls who altruistically feed them dime-sized fragments of manna.

I glance back over at the pile of rose petals on Zuzu's nightstand. All that's missing is a stem and some floral glue. I ponder the ailing, fictional Zuzu Bailey, the flower she receives as a reward from school.

My Zuzu's index finger finds another fowl on the page. *What about B-L-A-C-K-B-I-R-D?*

Blackbird singing in the dead of night… I whisper-sing in a nauseating imitation of Paul McCartney that would have the former Beatle performing cartwheels in his crypt had he truly died all those years ago. Zuzu looks up at me, her brow furrowed.

Do elementary school teachers ever give pupils flowers as rewards anymore, or is that completely make-believe in the first place? I recall that the reward system from my own early school experiences always consisted of shiny star stickers in an assortment of rainbow colors. Such cheap tokens of student accomplishment recorded various achievements such as clean desks, clear, crisp penmanship, and an untarnished attendance record. My teachers also awarded the occasional quarter-sized scratch-and-sniff sticker that held any number of captive aromas—pine, cinnamon, peppermint–magically released by the proud, anxious workings of the tiny nail on the index finger of a child's hand. When I was the eager recipient of such treasures, I recall receiving strawberry stickers, evergreen tree stickers, ice cream cone stickers…

And flower stickers. My mind drifts back to Zuzu Bailey's rose petals.

When I was a kid, I longed for a prize akin to them, the very ones that the fictional Zuzu's suicidal father George deftly pretends to reattach to his fictional daughter's drooping rose, employing imaginary paste and paternal, black and white sleight of hand, pocketing the fragile flower fragments beyond her gaze.

Deciding to ignore my previous non sequitur about Paul McCartney and his blackbird, Zuzu continues her line of questioning. *How about N-I-G-H-T-I-N-G-A-L-E?*

Nope. Harmless.

What about V-U-L-T-U-R-E? They eat dead meat.

I've heard that, too, I answer, itching to finish the book in hopes of making a hasty, surreptitious exit when her eyes are closed so that I can still catch the ending of my beloved movie in peace downstairs. I immediately become ashamed at such blatant, momentary selfishness. Dads are not supposed to act this way.

Daddy, do all birds eat dead meat?

My mind races. How many types of birds *do* feast on road kill?

No. A lot of them eat worms and bird seed, I say.

You can't script life, Jules.

Sure you can, Julie. Watch me.

But then you lose the spontaneity.

Too much spontaneity is chaos.

Chaos is life.

Then life needs to change. John Lennon once said, "We create our own reality."

John Lennon is dead.

No he isn't. He lives on through his music. People the world over are still listening to his recordings. His voice, his soul, still lives.

But that's all an illusion, Jules. It's electronic impulses recorded onto tape.

That doesn't matter to me.

I've watched *It's a Wonderful Life* countless times and have often regretted that Bedford Falls, the Baileys' place of residence in the picture, is an imaginary creation, nothing more than a long, elaborate set, dismantled ages ago no doubt, the parts of which were spread out across numerous Hollywood backlots as if scattered by a *Wizard of Oz*ish cyclone and reconstructed at random in order to appease the ongoing appetite of the old Tinseltown moviemaking machinery.

Daddy, do all birds eat dead meat?

My mind races. How many types of birds *do* feast on road kill?

No. A lot of them eat worms and bird seed, I say.

My thoughts continue to circle the track. I wish there were some way to convey to everyone that to me fictional characters are more real than real people and that I can visit and re-visit not only the objective and exterior lives of these characters but the interiors of fictional people's minds as well in a way that you simply can't do vis-à-vis actual flesh-and-blood people. And really will anyone at any given point in the future ever be able to read the minds of real people besides?

I long to walk down Bedford Falls' snow-plastered main drag, gaze in wonder at the Bailey Building and Loan, sit across from George at the public library and discuss architecture and the meaning of life. At long last, I let myself go...

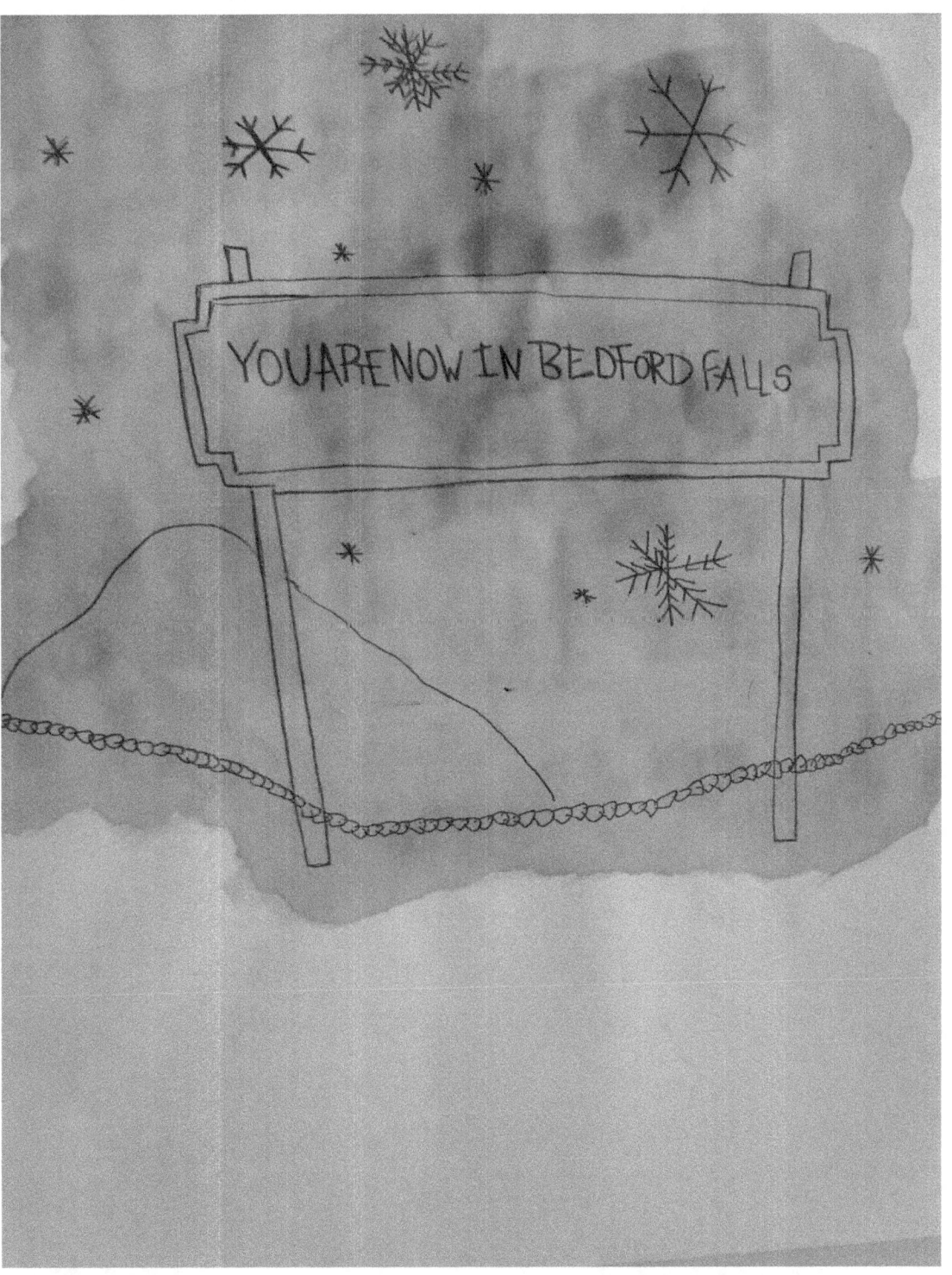

FADE IN—INT. BEDFORD FALLS LIBRARY—NIGHT

GEORGE and JULES sit across from each other. Various books
and magazines are scattered in front of GEORGE, some open,
some closed. In front of JULES is a blank yellow legal
pad. JULES holds a pen out as if ready to take notes.

>   JULES
>
>   George, I know how it is to forever be
>
>   chasing your dreams. For me it's like
>
>   hopelessly sprinting down the tracks after
>
>   a train that's just left the station and
>
>   tripping and falling over the railroad
>
>   ties.

>   GEORGE
>
>   I have my frustrations as well, Jules. I've
>
>   come to accept that I'll forever be trapped in
>
>   movies like this one. They're chock full of
>
>   clichés. Yet even clichés can be cracked open
>
>   to reveal kernels of truth. What are your
>
>   dreams, Jules?

JULES

My dreams are clichés. I want my loved ones
and myself to be safe and content. Maybe
"content" isn't the word I'm looking for.
Maybe I mean "fulfilled."

GEORGE

Go on.

JULES

I want to strike that precarious balance
between meeting my needs and the needs of
those I care for without my own needs taking
over so much, thereby transforming me into
some kind of jackass.

GEORGE

"Real" people like you enjoy characters like
me because we're closed, complete, finished.
We make mistakes yet tend to resolve them in
the nick of time within two hours or so.

                    JULES

I have to admit that I do envy you your

immortality. And the fact that legions of

people across time and geographical distance

continue to care about you and your doings,

even the most mundane ones, for the simple

reason that they're preserved on film and

projected onto a screen.

                    GEORGE

It's all an illusion, my friend. Shadows

and flickering light.

JULES riffles through the architectural books and magazines
on the table. He holds up an open volume that displays a
photograph of a gleaming skyscraper.

                    JULES

Do you ever regret that you were never able

to build one of these?

                    GEORGE

You and I will never know. I never appeared

in a sequel. But allow me to show you

something.

GEORGE holds up a children's picture book of assorted animals…

...Do people eat bird seed?

I'm not sure. I've never tried it myself. I don't think so. No.

I firmly press my fingertips against my temples and rub. Something I am having trouble identifying is wreaking havoc on my responses.

Why not?

I don't know, really. Because birds are supposed to.

I would love to break an upper window on the front of the abandoned abode at 320 Sycamore with an expertly-aimed rock before George and his wife-to-be Mary take residence there. Maybe *after* the couple is proud homeowners of the drafty place, I can stoop and feel the worn runner on the staircase, affectionately lift the ornamental wooden ball that caps the end of the balustrade at the bottom stair, bring it to my own lips and kiss it again and again as George has done.

I feel that if it's possible, George and I can lounge for hours at the Bailey kitchen table, debating the three most exciting sounds in the world: anchor chains, plane motors, train whistles, or some other auditory gem George hasn't yet imagined. I know I could out-think George's Uncle Billy on such a topic. A third grader could do *that*, come to think of it.

Why can't I break myself from the habit of looking off into the nostalgic distance of my own past, ignoring my present existence?

...INT. BAILEY KITCHEN—MORNING

JULES and GEORGE are sipping mugs of coffee at a table.

> JULES
>
> The three best sounds in the world, you ask?
> Side Two of Abbey Road, moans of passion during
> lovemaking, and the words "I love you, Daddy"
> from my daughter, in descending order. Come to
> think of it, sex and the Beatles tie for
> second.

> GEORGE
>
> That certainly beats the devil out of Uncle
> Billy's favorite sounds. "Breakfast is served...
> lunch is served...dinner is served."

…George and I could have mourned the loss of dreams. We were destined to treasure the oft-underappreciated gifts of friendship and fatherhood together as friends and fathers ourselves…

Does it taste bad?

Does *what* taste bad, honey?

Daddy. You're not listening to me. Bird seed.

I really don't know. Like I said, I've never had it. It probably tastes a lot like Grape Nuts without the milk, but on a much tinier scale, like gravel or sand.

I realize at the end of my rambling that it is the most mental muscle I've ever flexed on this particular topic. Squeezing my eyes shut until I hear ersatz thunder in my ears, I will the images crowding my mind onto the behavior of Zuzu, longing to regale her with tales of the gardenful of roses that wait behind her eyelids.

"Youth is wasted on the wrong people!" an aging, balding, black-and-white cigar-chomping porch denizen blurts in the movie. How sad and true. Jimmy Stewart and Donna Reed continue to toss stones at the window of the old estate that resides between my ears, the very same one that will one day house the Bailey family, two actors not realizing that their shared moment on a Hollywood soundstage will last an eternity, one moment captured on film by the factory-like efficiency of the studio system, remembered and cherished long after Reed and Stewart became dust lining their own coffins beneath feet of solid cemetery soil.

Can we get some?

Can we get what, honey?

Bird seed.

We'll see. Don't you want to finish the story?

Sure. Do cats eat bird seed?

No. They eat cat food. And dogs eat dog food, and fish eat fish food, I respond. I want to pre-empt any imminent questions, yet Zuzu's infinite inventiveness, her bottomless well of interrogation, is winning out.

I've always been the type of person who is much more apt to cry at movies than at events from my own life. Such "real" events are supposed to house their own sort of self-proscribed significance. Lately, I've rekindled the habit of keeping a small writing journal, which I haven't practiced since college. I'm a man who hasn't written anything creative down since those years as an official scholar, but now I find myself losing track of time in a chair, scribbling cursive like mad in a spiral notebook the size of an Uno card.

Michelangelo had the Sistine Chapel ceiling, Ray Kinsella had his ballpark in a sea of cornstalks. Perhaps I should set out to build Bedford Falls. Wouldn't that be a sight? What the hell would the neighbors think?

I see myself stalking the aisles of Home Depot, lined as they are with shelves full of all manner of 2x4, screw, nail, hammer, and the like. Would I be there to find materials with which to re-build Bedford Falls, or would I be there for said materials to build a mere deck on the back of my home?

My consciousness phases back into the confines of Zuzu's bedroom, and I will certainty and closure into the life that she and I share, but my hands grope in my pockets, feeling nothing but a grocery store receipt and a miniscule ball of lint.

Children don't choose to be born. They aren't afforded the luxury of selecting their own parents. They never ask for life's pain. I immediately think of that moment in *The Catcher in the Rye* when Holden Caulfield describes how the Indians in the canoe, the Eskimos, the birds flying south, the deer drinking from the water hole, and other display items in the museum's glass display case will stay the same while those visiting the museum will be different somehow whenever they return. I recall feeling the character's wistful envy coursing down the pages of Salinger's novel…

Daddy, did you hear me? I asked if dogs and cats and fish get sick if they eat bird seed.

Probably, sweetheart.

Daddy, please pay attention to me.

I know that the constant mental exercises that comprise much of my life are considered a waste of time by some, Julie certainly included. For them, they are the equivalent of running on a treadmill and making no real forward progress. It's true that on the surface my random thoughts lead to no concrete destination in particular, but I believe my musings nevertheless burn away the fat in which the significance of my past experiences are encased to yield meaty clarity.

Despite such self-assurances, however, I can't help but wonder how much time I'll continue to spend searching in the cluttered present for the emotions I experienced when I was younger. Occasionally I can detect such feelings when I revisit places that have even the slightest significance to my past. Too many of these places, Bedford Falls included, exist only within the confines of some fictional realm.

How will I ever be able to fully protect Zuzu from all the horrors of the real world? How can I protect her from what's going on between Julie and me? I can hardly handle myself. What the hell kind of parent am I?

I feel a rush of sadness brush below my shoulders, and the cynicism that always lies dormant just underneath my skin immediately bursts forth. I think of George Bailey's conversation with the villainous Mr. Potter late in the film, the one during which Potter attempts to bamboozle Bailey into working for him for a much higher salary than the measly one to which he is accustomed. Like George, I am constantly in danger of falling victim to false, base, fictional temptations…

INT. POTTER'S OFFICE—AFTERNOON

POTTER sits in a wheelchair behind his desk. JULES stands before him, having refused the expensive cigar POTTER has alternately waved and caressed in front of him.

                         POTTER

          What, man? Do you really imagine that

          your daughter will stay sweet and innocent?

          Pure? Hah!

                         JULES

          Did you ever have kids, Potter?

                         POTTER

          Me? Kids? You kidding?

                         JULES

          That's good to hear. The one mental

          image I don't need in my head is you

          fornicating with somebody.

                         POTTER

          Look, wiseacre. I'm greed incarnate,

          do you understand? Condensed evil.

                         (MORE)

POTTER (contd.)

I'm the guy hiding in shadows, waiting
for an opportunity to pounce on the pure,
to entice the innocent, to violate the
virtuous. I'm not interested in your
offspring in particular. Yet perhaps I
am. What I'm saying is, it's not the
actual done deed that's the worst. It's
the anticipation, the fear of Zuzu turning
to the dark side, experiencing pain and
heartache. Am I right?

JULES

I don't know what you're talking about.

POTTER

Having some problems on the home front,
aren't we, Jules? Marriage in tatters,
torn to shreds, that sort of thing? Poor
little Zuzu receiving info on a "need-to-
know" basis?

JULES

I don't want to hear this. Go to hell, Potter.

POTTER

If by "hell" you mean the "real world,"
I'm afraid I cannot go there with you.
The road you traveled to get here can
only be traversed in one direction. This
isn't The Last Action Hero or The Purple
Rose of Cairo, lad. I'm merely a character,
a Hollywood hack's creation, and am powerless
in that regard. Besides, you know that I'm
right.

JULES

Yes. No.

A 1940s-era candlestick phone on POTTER'S desk rings.
POTTER lifts the handset to his ear and speaks into the
mouthpiece.

POTTER

Yes? Yes, he's here. I'll get him for
you. (His eyes bore into JULES as he
smirks.) It's for you, Jules. It's your
wife. It's Julie.

JULES

No, dammit. I don't want to talk to her...

... Daddy? Who are you talking to? You shouldn't say 'dammit.'

I didn't, honey. I mean, I shouldn't. I won't.

I think of the scene in *It's a Wonderful Life* during which George Bailey, despondent, sits at Martini's bar, lips twisted in agony, teeth bared, his hands clasped in desperate hope, praying aloud to a God whose existence he doubts.

What do clouds taste like?

I once more pull myself back into the present. I say, I don't know. I've never tasted one.

You taste clouds in heaven, you know.

Is that so?

Yeah, because people live on clouds in heaven.

I think of Clarence the angel from *It's a Wonderful Life* and offer up a silent prayer, even going so far as to address the Almighty at the outset just as Bailey does during his moments of emotional turmoil...

EXT. BRIDGE - NIGHT

JULES and CLARENCE stand at the edge of the bridge on
which GEORGE earlier contemplated suicide. They gaze over
the edge at the turbulent water below.

                         JULES

         Dear God in heaven.

                       CLARENCE

         What is it that you want, Jules?

                         JULES

         I just want Zuzu to be protected,

         especially from her parents' problems

         and foibles. I want her to not

         experience an overabundance of loss

         and disappointment, and I want the cup

         that holds the experiences of her life

         to overflow with promise and contentment.

         I want life to be simpler.

CLARENCE

Jules, I've been an angel for quite
some time. I'm nearly two hundred and
ninety-three years old. I've picked up
some things over the years, and I can
tell you this. Especially at your
relatively young age, life's sudden,
unexpected hurdles can cow you like nothing
else. Actually, the hurdles are relatively
easy to hop. It's the brick walls that leave
all manner of scars and bruises and scrapes.

JULES

Please don't take this the wrong way,
Clarence. I realize that you're a guardian
angel and all, but I'm having a hard time
understanding what the hell you're telling
me.

CLARENCE

"Hell" is such a horrific word for an angel,
even a fictional one, to hear. But have faith,
Jules.

(MORE)

CLARENCE (contd.)

Have faith that you've given things your best shot and that your Zuzu will survive. She will be able to follow your example and successfully walk the scary tightrope between innocence and experience,and if she happens to lose her balance, unconditional love and understanding provide ideal cushions for an accidental fall.

JULES

I can't believe it, but I actually think I understand. Clarence, when you're back up there in the Great Beyond, tell Jimmy Stewart I said hello. I wish he was still around, walking the earth. And tell William Blake I said "Hey," too, while you're at it. The whole "innocence versus experience" thing, you know? I took a Romantic poetry class in college way back when. It's a long story that only a recovering English major can tell. Let's get off this bridge, Clarence.

As JULES and CLARENCE walk towards one end of the bridge, JULIE appears out of the shadows and steps directly into their path.

JULIE

Oh no you don't. It's not that easy. Real
life is never that easy.

JULES

It doesn't have to be as hard as you make it
out to be.

JULIE

That's easy to say when you make every effort
to constantly escape it.

JULES

That's garbage. I always eventually come
back.

JULIE

Not often enough for me, I'm afraid.

JULES

What the hell are you even doing here? This
is my daydream, not yours!

JULIE

It's nighttime, Jules, and you should be
reading to your daughter.

                    JULES

No, you should, *we* should be reading to our

daughter.

                    JULIE

Look, Jules. I'm a good person. I'm not the

bitch that you make me out to be. I've taken

care of you, of *us* during our whole marriage.

And I've also taken care of Zuzu. It's

always been *my* burden to take care of the

practical things that just have to be done.

CLARENCE, who has been standing off to the side during the
altercation thus far, steps forward to speak.

                    CLARENCE

  Excuse me, Julie. Allow me to introduce

  myself-

                    JULIE

I know who you are, you idiotic,

pretend bastard. I've been dragged

kicking and screaming in front of the

TV to watch your movie every frigging year.

CLARENCE

Now, there is really no reason to be saucy

and rude-

JULIE suddenly grabs CLARENCE by the lapels of his over-
coat. She drags him to the middle of the bridge. All this
time CLARENCE looks skyward, his hands supine, as if his
is a necessary sacrifice. JULIE throws him over the side.
There is a splash, a smattering of bubbles across the surface of the icy water, and then silence below the still-
turbulent waves. JULES runs to the middle of the bridge.

JULES

My God, Julie. You just killed an angel!

JULIE

It's over, Jules. We have to go through

with this. We have got to tell Zuzu.

JULES

We will. I can't. I just don't know.

JULES tries to embrace JULIE, but she pushes him away and
steps back.

                    JULIE

We can tell her tonight. I can come over.

I'll just call you, and we can get Zuzu on

the phone. We'll do this together. Wait. No. I

want to be home for it. We'll do it

face-to-face.

                    JULES

Okay. If you think that is best.

JULES glances over the side at the barren surface of the
choppy water as JULIE leaves the bridge. He looks in the
direction from which she has just exited the scene.

                    JULES

She said "home." WWGD? What Would George Do?

JULES exits the scene, trailing JULIE…

…Daddy? Zuzu gently shakes me.

Yes, honey?

You were out of it for a long time. I've been trying to wake you up. I'm tired. I wanna sleep too.

Okay, pumpkin. That makes two of us.

I close the picture book.

Daddy?

Yes, honey?

I love you, Daddy.

I love you too, precious. More than you know.

'Night.

Zuzu has closed her eyes, and as I raise myself from the bed, I palm a handful of the potpourri petals that have spilled onto her dresser. Bending my head and cupping my hand over both nostrils, I inhale. The memory of the petals' fragrance, still encapsulated within them for years, manages to tickle and tug at my nostrils.

I slip the petals into the pocket of my jeans in deliberate imitation of George Bailey. In the process I crush them by accident to miniscule particles that will turn to a fine dust if I'm not careful. No matter. Later I can transfer as many of them as I can to a Ziploc baggie and place the preserved petals into a box filled with what other people would construe to be a meaningless, random assortment of odds and ends but for me are mementos that represent significant episodes of my past and present existence.

I hope that Zuzu and I, running through the garden together hand in hand, will be careful not to accidentally trip and trample over the roses on our shared path toward the horizon that lines our dreamscape, however threatening the skies will turn.

I want to tell Julie, Zuzu, all of them all of this and more, but I feel hog-tied by the fact that I will never surpass George Bailey's abilities as a father. George, for me, being the ideal human being and all.

I start to head for the hallway but stop at the threshold and turn around.

Honey?

Yes, Daddy?

Would you like to come downstairs with me to watch the end of *It's a Wonderful Life?*

I like Spongebob better, Daddy. He's in color. And he's funny.

Okay, honey.

I hate old movies.

You really shouldn't. They're classy and refined.

I don't know what 'classy' and 'refined' is.

Never mind, sweets.

The lightning and thunder continue to crash beyond the thin protective layer of glass that is Zuzu's window. I descend the stairs alone. The phone rings and I answer. At the same time the doorbell rings. I leave footsteps of amniotic fluid in my wake as I stagger forward.

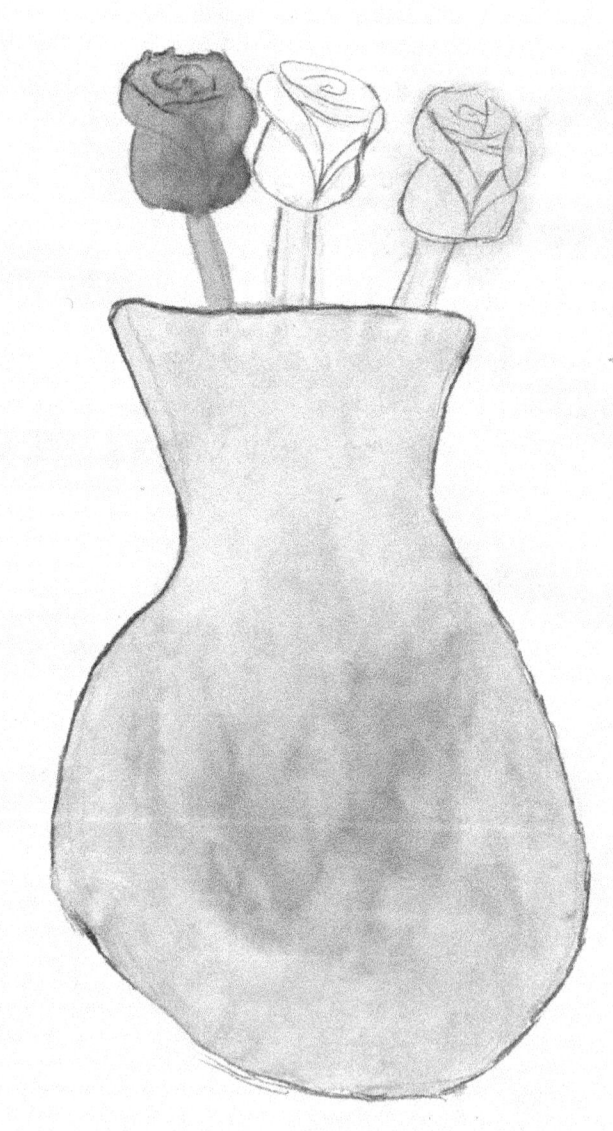

—FADE—

Jeff Jarot is a writer who teaches high school English. He holds a BA in English from Illinois Wesleyan University, a BA in English Education and MA in English from Illinois State University, and an MA in English from Northern Illinois University. Jarot's short story "Home Movies" appeared in *Festival Writer*. An essay on David Foster Wallace's short story "The Depressed Person" was also featured in the anthology *Normal 2014: Selected Works from The First Annual DFW Conference*. Jarot also recently presented an essay at the second annual David Foster Wallace Conference in Normal, Illinois in May 2015, in which he applied Wallace's ideas regarding television set forth in "E Unibus Pluram: Television and U.S. Fiction" to present-day social-networking. He lives in Plainfield, Illinois with his wife and three children.

www.ingramcontent.com/pod-product-compliance
Lightning Source LLC
Chambersburg PA
CBHW080820250626
47159CB00011B/3455